MYRO and the Tiger Moth

Belongs to ....

Also available...

Audio CD
Myro, The Smallest Plane In The World

Songs and Music CD

MYRO
The Smallest Plane In The World

Myro and the Tiger Moth
Book 3 from Series 1: Myro Goes to Australia

First published October 2010 by NickRose Ltd
www.nickrose.com
ISBN 978-1-907972-02-7

Myro's Team
Concept and Story: Nick Rose
Illustrations and Branding: Lucy Corrina Bourn
Designer: Sue Mason
Writer: Fiona Veitch Smith
Editor: Mary O'Riordan
Editorial Consultant: Samantha Mackintosh
Australian Consultant: Jane Massam
3D Consultancy: Jon Stuart and Sean Frisby
Project Management: Nick Rose
Continue the fun at www.myro.com

nr.
nickrose ltd

MYRO
and the
TIGER MOTH

Nick Rose

Myro the microlight
is the smallest plane
in the world!

He loves to fly in the
Australian Bush . . .

. . . but sometimes he likes to watch the clouds from the ground too.

One hot, sunny day Myro was all alone on the farm.
At least he thought he was.

Myro heard a deep cough from the barn.

Chugga, chugg, cough!

"Hello, is anybody there?" called Myro,
taxiing over to the rickety building.

"Go away," said a grumpy voice.

Myro looked through the gloom and saw the nose of an old Tiger Moth.

His paint was peeling away and his bolts and rivets were rusted. And, even sadder than that, he had no propeller or wings.

"Sorry to bother you, sir," said Myro.

"Sir?" said the old plane, sounding a little less cross.
"No one's called me sir since the Air Force!"

He creaked as he
rolled closer to Myro.
"My name's Tymo," he said.
"What's yours, little fella?"

"Myro! I'm from the UK.
Were you made there too?"

"No, mate. I'm one of the Australian
Tigers, built Down Under.
But you're not the first Brit I've met," said Tymo.
The old plane had a twinkle in his eye.

"When I was young I trained Pommy, Kiwi and Aussie fighter pilots to fly Vampire Jets," said Tymo proudly. "It was great – even the crashes."

"Crashes?" Myro shuddered.

Tymo laughed.
"Don't worry. Tiger Moths are easy to mend. We'd be flying again the next day!"

Tymo continued,
"Years later, I joined a flying circus."

"Crikey," said Myro, **"a circus!"**

"We used to perform acrobatics all around
Australia!" Tymo chuckled to himself as he
remembered the cheering crowds.

"But how did you end up here?" asked Myro.

Tymo frowned. "I was a crop duster for the farm, spraying fields. But now my spare parts are so hard to find, I can't fly any more."

The old Tiger Moth looked sad but – **prrfffffffffft!** – went a panel near his tail, making a rude noise. Both aircraft laughed as Tymo said, "Oops! Pardon me! Gotta watch me rivets – they keep popping off!"

With that a panel clanged to the ground and Tymo added, "I'm not sure how much longer I can keep it all together." And suddenly Myro and Tymo didn't feel like laughing any more.

That night, back at the Flying Club, Myro couldn't sleep.

"Gigi," he whispered. "I'm worried about
the old Tiger Moth. I want to help him fly again."

"Tymo?" mumbled Gigi sleepily. "He'll have to be restored first.
Why not speak to Ray at the aeroplane museum? I'm sure he'll help."

The next day Michael phoned Ray.

"Sorry, Myro, but Ray says he's
too busy to find the spare parts."

Myro was very upset.

"He's got to help!" he cried.
"Tymo's going to fall apart if no one fixes him!"

"Did I hear someone say Tymo?" asked Ray.

"Yes, Tymo, the Tiger Moth," Michael replied.

"Fair dinkum?" cried Ray. "He trained me to fly when I was a youngie! I'd do anything to help him!"

When Tymo heard the news, tears came into his eyes.

"Thanks, Myro. I thought everyone had forgotten me."

Over the next few months Ray put all his efforts into finding the parts needed to repair Tymo.

Ray found spare wings in Perth . . .

and bought new wood for the panels from Darwin . . .

and had a propeller made in Sydney.

Western Australia

Perth

Australia

Darwin

Northern Territory

Queensland

Cairns

Alice Springs

South Australia

Brisbane

New South Wales

Adelaide

Sydney

Canberra

ACT

Victoria

Melbourne

Tasmania

Hobart

In Alice Springs Ray had nice new leather cut for the seats . . .

Ray tracked down new wheels in Brisbane . . .

and finally Tymo's old engine was repaired in Melbourne.

But the next time Myro and Gigi were at the farm,
Michael came over looking worried.

"I've got bad news, Myro," he said. "Tymo can't be fixed.
We can't find him an instrument panel."

Tiger Moth
Speed must not
exceed 139 knots
No Smoking

Height

"But there **must** be one somewhere," said Myro, tears welling up.

"I'm sorry, but they're very rare," said Michael.
"Tymo will have to be scrapped."

"Noooo!" cried Myro.

Devastated, Myro spun off to Tymo's old barn.
"Oh, Myro, I'm so sorry," said Gigi, trying to comfort her friend.
"I shouldn't have got Tymo's hopes up," sobbed Myro.

"It's not your fault,"
Gigi replied kindly.
"You tried your
hardest."

"My hardest wasn't good enough," whispered Myro, rolling away.

Suddenly there was the sound of breaking glass under his front wheel.

"What's that?" called Gigi.

Crack!
Crunch!

Myro looked down and saw a wooden panel with round dials, poking out of a dusty sack.

"What's that?" wondered Myro out loud.

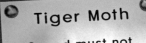

Tiger Moth

Speed must not exceed 139 knots

No Smoking

"Strewth!" cried Michael, walking into the barn. "That looks like Tymo's instrument panel!"

"Oh, WOW!" yelled Myro. "This means that Tymo won't be scrapped!"

"Only if we get to the museum quickly," said Michael.

"*All right!*" cried Gigi. **"Let's go!"**

Myro and Gigi flew at top
speed to the museum.

Ray was ready to start taking Tymo apart.

The Tiger Moth was
the saddest he'd
ever been.

He'd given up all hope.

"STOP!"
yelled Myro, with a
screech of his tyres.

Michael handed over the instrument panel.

"You beauty!"cried Ray, looking at it with amazement.
"You've saved him! *You've saved Tymo!*"

The old plane couldn't believe his ears!
"Are you saying I can fly again?"

"Too right! And I bags the first flight!" chuckled Ray.
"We'll have ya looping the loop in next to no time, mate!"

"Yessss!" yelled Myro and Gigi.

Tymo laughed so loud Myro thought the old plane might pop another rivet.

But with his instruments back the old Tiger Moth would soon be as good as new!